ISBN (Paperback): 979-8-9881073-8-5
ISBN (eBook): 979-8-9881073-7-8

To my daughters who love art.

Love,

Mom

Thank you to the Artist who
believed in me.

Jonah the dolphin, his best friend Mel the starfish, and his pet sea turtle, were blowing bubbles.

Plop!

Something dropped into the water.

Anthony, the shark, was swimming by, and they all looked at it.

"What is it?" asked Jonah.

The shark said, "It came from above, but I scared it away."

Freckles the whale was on his way to school.

"Hey, what is that?" he asked.

"We don't know. Let's take it to school for show and tell," Mel said.

"Good idea!" said Jonah.

At the sea ground, Jonah showed it to his friends.

"Oh!" said Oscar, the seahorse.

At the same time, Jack and Diane, the twin crabs, said, "What is it?"

Gina, the octopus, said, "That looks like trash."

"It's not trash; it's beautiful," said Jonah.

Jonah went to his favorite teacher, Miss Jillyfish, and showed it to her.

Mr. Ray came to see too. But Mr. Scrimp was in a bad mood; he said, "What is that? We do not want trash."

Ms. Jillyfish said, "Oh dear, that is a painting. Up there, they call it art."

When Jonah got home, he was
very excited.

"Mom, I am going to do painting and
make art."

The mother dolphin said, "The things
above the water do that. We cannot
go up there, Jonah; they will catch you.
And I will never see you again."

Jonah put all the stuff he found on his desk in his room.

He was going to learn how to paint.

Who could teach him?

That night he had a dream about a beautiful painting.

Jonah and Mel went to the rainbow school of fish the next day. They made art out of coral.

Jonah asked Ms. Greene if he could paint there.

The teacher fish was happy to help them.

When Jonah squeezed the paint, it turned into blobs and floated up.

Oh no!

He made a huge mess.

Jonah was covered in paint. Anthony asked, "What's wrong, buddy?"

He said, "I tried to paint and made a yucky mess."

"Hmm...We should go up there and see how the thing does it," said the shark.

So, they went to the top of the water and watched the thing.

It was holding the brush and using the paint. There was something it was putting the paint on.

Jonah did not know that paint is put on a canvas.

They went back to the rainbow school of fish. Ms. Greene found some flat coral for Jonah to paint on.

Jonah tried to hold the paintbrush.

Again, the paint squirted, then floated up in the water and made a mess.

"Oh no!" they all said.

The others in the sea did not understand Jonah. They were talking about him.

"Why does he want to make trash?"

Dolphins don't paint.

They did not believe in Jonah.

The shark, dolphin, and starfish went back above to see the thing.

When it saw them watching, it chased them.

Oh no, was it going to catch and eat them!

Anthony and Mel swam away fast, but Jonah looked at the thing and froze.

The thing was saying something
to the dolphin.

One day, the thing came back, and
Jonah saw that it brought a canvas,
more paint, and a paintbrush.

It waved to the dolphin to get closer.

The thing put the paintbrush in its mouth and moved its head up and down.

Aww. He had to put the paintbrush in his mouth!

Jonah tried it, and the thing held out the canvas. The dolphin dipped the paintbrush and watercolor into the water and moved his head up and down in circles.

Oh Wow! He was painting!

The thing smiled at Jonah and went away.

Jonah was happy; he had done what he dreamed about.

Then a surprise came, the thing came back, but there were more things this time.

They held paintbrushes and waited for Jonah to paint for them.

The Artist believed in Jonah and liked his paintings.

When others in the sea heard about this, they went to watch Jonah.

The dolphin would swim to the top of the water, and below, they watched.

"Paint Jonah Paint," they cheered.

I hope you enjoyed the book and that it encourages you to share love and chase dreams.

For more inspirational books in the series, visit: www.vatsanabooks.com.

Printed in the USA
CPSIA information can be obtained
at www.ICGtesting.com
JSHW041540230923
48887JS00009BA/63

9 798988 107385